WAITING FOR NOAH

BY SHULAMITH LEVEY OPPENHEIM

ILLUSTRATED BY LILLIAN HOBAN

Harper & Row, Publishers

Waiting for Noah
Text copyright © 1990 by Shulamith Levey Oppenheim
Illustrations copyright © 1990 by Lillian Hoban

Library of Congress Cataloging-in-Publication Data
Oppenheim, Shulamith Levey.
   Waiting for Noah / by Shulamith Levey Oppenheim ; pictures by
Lillian Hoban.
       p.   cm.
   "A Charlotte Zolotow book."
   Summary: Noah hears the story of the day that his grandmother
waited for him to be born.
   ISBN 0-06-024633-2 : $ — ISBN 0-06-024634-0 (lib. bdg.) : $
   [1. Birthdays—Fiction.   2. Grandmothers—Fiction.]—I. Hoban,
Lillian, ill.   II. Title.
PZ7.0618Wai 1990   89-35561
[E]—dc20   CIP
                                                            AC

Printed in the U.S.A. All rights reserved.
        1 2 3 4 5 6 7 8 9 10
                   First Edition

For Layne and Daniel, Noah's parents;
Nancy and Bill and Poppy and Nana,
Noah's grandparents; and
the rest of the family, all of whom were
Waiting for Noah

S.L.O.

For Benjamin, from his Safta
L.H.

Noah pops a thumb-size berry in his mouth. The juice, red sweet and warm, runs down his chin.

Nana takes a large square handkerchief and wipes his face. She smiles.

"The day your daddy called to say that you were on your way into this world, I put the clipper in the pocket of my jeans and walked beyond the fence, to prune the ends of berry canes. The air was winter cold."

Today in the berry patch the sun is very warm.

"And then?" Noah asks. He loves to hear it time and time again.
"Tell me again, Nana, what happened next?"

"And then I had a conversation with the cats.

"'When summer comes,' I said to them, 'we'll pick the berries warm and sweet, the baby and I.'"

She turned to Noah. "The baby that would be you."

She kisses Noah's cheek.

"And then you baked?" Noah asks.

"That's right, I baked."

"I filled the cookie jar with disks, molasses-brown,
the raisins fattening out their sides.

"And while the cookies cooled, I shined the pots
along the wall. And even then, it seemed as if
the clock had stopped by half."

Nana moves deep into the patch and Noah follows, prickles leaving scratch marks on his arms.

He tugs at Nana's picking can, which hangs around her neck.

"Next, Nana! What happened *next*?"

"Well, evening came. And still…you hadn't come."

Nana tips her head a little to the side.

"So I dreamed on. I thought…

"…we'll listen to the peepers on the hill
and watch the glow of fireflies
and count the last chirps of the birds
before they tuck their heads beneath their wings.

"We'll bicycle…

"…and walk the forest path up to the pond

"and read about the seven swans, the happy prince and…"

Noah gives a hop.

"And why the sea is salt!" he shouts.

"And why the sea is salt," repeats his nana softly.

And then, right there among the brambly canes, Nana kneels and takes Noah's face between her hands.

"And soon," she whispers, "it was the middle of the night.

"Your daddy called and…"

Noah thinks his chest will burst!

"Your daddy said, 'Nana! Is this *Noah's* Nana?'"

Noah throws his arms around her neck.
"Oh yes," they answer in a hug.
"Oh yes, it is!"